Kazuo Iwamura

Good-bye, WINTER!
Hello, SPRING!

North
South

Good-bye, winter! Hello, spring!
What will warmer weather bring?

Mick woke up and said, "Oh no!
What happened to the pretty snow?"

Their father said with a sigh,
"The snow returns to the sky."

David Henry Wilson was born in London in 1937. He is a retired university lecturer, playwright, and novelist, and has written many children's books, including the popular Jeremy James series. He is widowed, has two sons, a daughter, three grandsons, and lots of chocolate. He lives in Taunton, England.

The children saw the clouds up high.
"Look! The snow's back in the sky!"

Molly said, "I hear dripping over there!
Come and see. It's everywhere!"
Her brothers asked, "What's that sound?"
"Little streams—they're all around."

Not long after, it became quite clear:
The snow was beginning to disappear.
As Mick and Mack and Molly looked,
It turned into a babbling brook.

They shouted, "I wonder where the water goes?"
Into a stream–*WHOOSH!*–it flows.
And in the water what did they see?
The floating trunk of a fallen tree . . .
Mack jumped on and said, "Come quick!"
"Wait for me!" shouted brother Mick.
Molly said, "Suppose we fall . . ."
But onto the log she carefully crawled.

Tap, tip, tap, trrr . . .
Came the snow-melted water.
It sang as it joined into one stream.
A nightingale's voice trembled like a dream.
The three of them on their tree-trunk boat
Merrily away began to float.

But after a while they began to think,
What if our floating log should sink?
The water gushed into the river.
The sight and sound made all three shiver.
The melting snow—down it poured.
How they wished they'd stayed indoors!

They held on tight. Their log it snaked
Out into a great big lake.

Some kindly ducks came swimming by.
"Help! Help!" the little squirrels cried.
Each duck took one of them on its back.
"We'll get you safely home," they said. *Quack, quack!*

With duck feathers softer than the tree,
The siblings sat quite comfortably.
Over the water those ducks did glide.
They couldn't have had a smoother ride.
"Where does the melted snow go?" asked the three.
The ducks said, "To a river and then to the sea.
In spring, the snow goes back into the earth
And the sea and the sky—it's a time of rebirth.
We ducks too will go back north.
Every year we gather to fly back and forth."

Then it was time for the ducks to depart.
"Thank you, dear ducks!" the kids said from the heart.
"Let's meet here next fall!" said the ducks, flying high.
And soon they disappeared into the blue sky.
"Our dear ducks are like snow," Mick said with a sigh.
"When the spring comes, they return to the sky."

Their mom and dad said, "Where did you go?
We thought you got lost in the melting snow!"

"Mom, Dad, did you know?
The water in this pond is melted snow.
It runs farther and farther and out to the sea.
Then it goes back to the sky to be snow again, see?"

Their parents laughed and said, "That's right.
Our three kids are brave and bright.
Now, who's hungry?"

"Me!" "Me!" "Me!"

"We brought acorns from our tree.
Let's have a picnic, then we'll sing:
'Good-bye, winter! Hello, spring!'"

Read all of Mick, Mack, and Molly's adventures:

Hooray for Spring!
It's spring, and the world is full of new leaves, cherry blossoms,
and hungry baby birds. Mick, Mack, and Molly can see that caterpillars
like to eat leaves, and bees like nectar from blossoms, but what can
they feed a hungry young chick?

Hooray for Summer!
When a little bird warns Mick, Mack, and Molly that a storm
is coming, the siblings take shelter in a small cave, where they meet
new friends—two little mice and a small rabbit—and wait out
the summer storm.

Hooray for Fall!
Mama has a surprise for Mick, Mack, and Molly: three bright red
sweaters to keep them warm. Imagine their surprise when they find
that everything in the autumn woods—the leaves, the berries,
and the setting sun—is red too!

Hooray for Snow!
Overnight, something magical has happened: SNOW! The world
is covered in white. Mick, Mack, and Molly can't wait to get out in it.
Will Mama and Papa like it as much?
This perfect day in the snow will spark memories and anticipation.

Every season is beautiful with Mick, Mack, and Molly!